Litterbug Doug

Illustrated by
Alexandra Colombo

Written by
Ellie Bethel

In a beautiful valley,
in the shade of a hill,
was a clean little town
that was full of goodwill.

But the quaint little town had a problem to face for on top of the hill stood a mountain **of waste!**

And who was the culprit? who was the **thug?** It was **lonely** and lazy-boned...

Litterbug Doug!

His house was a rubbish dump,
full of old stuff,
that was rotting and mouldy
and smelly enough
to make your eyes water
(the pong was so **strong**)
but Doug didn't think
he'd done anything wrong.

And his only real friends,
were a hundred odd rats
(except for two lazy
and fat tabby cats).

From alone on his throne
Doug thoughtlessly threw
all manner of litter.
And so the pile grew.

A rotting banana,
some **mouldy** old cheese,
faulty fridge freezers,
and **smashed** up TVs.
A table, a tandem,
an old three piece suite,
all kinds of old rubbish
was hurled on the heap.

And then to the joy
of the hundred odd rats,
Doug even got rid of
his two tabby cats!

The cats were so fat
that they made the dump fall...

...and down
came the rubbish heap,
rats, cats and all!

But then something happened
that none could explain.
It wasn't a bird and it wasn't a plane.

A green-caped crusader
stupendously swooped,
descending to Earth
with a great loop-the-loop!

"**Litterbug Doug,**" said our green-hero, Michael,

But Doug just retorted,
"I won't make amends.
I don't need these people.
The rats are my friends!"

"Of course not!" said Michael.

"With all hands on deck,
we can work hard together
to save you just yet!"

They formed a big chain
from Doug's dump to Michael,
to sort out the rubbish
and what to recycle,

and soon all the town
was so neat and pristine,
the only thing left was to...

...give Doug
a clean!

So now he was neater
and no longer smelled
they gave him a job
at which he excelled.

So watch out!
Don't litter
or drop one
small piece,

Doug's there in a flash...

...he's the Litter Police!

To my super-siblings, Andrew and Jacqui...
thanks for all your super-support!
E.B

For Mummy, Gnome, Pepi, Kay and Enrico
who help me every day to become
a better person

A.C

First published in 2009
by Meadowside Children's Books
185 Fleet Street London EC4A 2HS
www.meadowsidebooks.com
www.cpre.org.uk

A CIP catalogue record for this book
is available from the British Library
10 9 8 7 6 5 4 3 2
Printed in china